Note: All activities in this book should be performed with adult supervision. Children should not use potentially dangerous tools or household equipment. Common sense and care are essential to the conduct of any and all activities whether described in this book or not. Neither the author nor the publisher assumes any responsibility for any injuries or damages arising from any activities.

KINGFISHER
An imprint of Kingfisher Publications Plc
New Penderel House, 283–288 High Holborn
London WC1V 7HZ
www.kingfisherpub.com

First published in Sweden by Alfabeta Bokförlag
First published in the UK by Kingfisher 2006
This edition published 2007 for Index Books Ltd
1 3 5 7 9 10 8 6 4 2

A CIP catalogue record for this book is available from the British Library.

ISBN: 978 0 7534 1205 3

Printed in Taiwan
INDEX/0407/SHENS/(SGCH)/158MA/F

Harvey the Decorator

Lars Klinting

KINGFISHER

Harvey is going to do some decorating! He wants to paint the cupboard. Chip is so excited! He is going to help. But what is Harvey going to put in the cupboard once it's been decorated? He doesn't know yet.
Never mind, painting is fun!

First, Harvey needs to take out the shelves and unscrew the doors, so it's easy to paint everything. What colour is the cupboard going to be, Harvey?

Harvey hasn't decided yet – it's hard to pick one colour. Chip has an idea. They can use lots of different colours. That way, they don't have to choose!

Harvey looks under the bench and takes out

a roll of paper

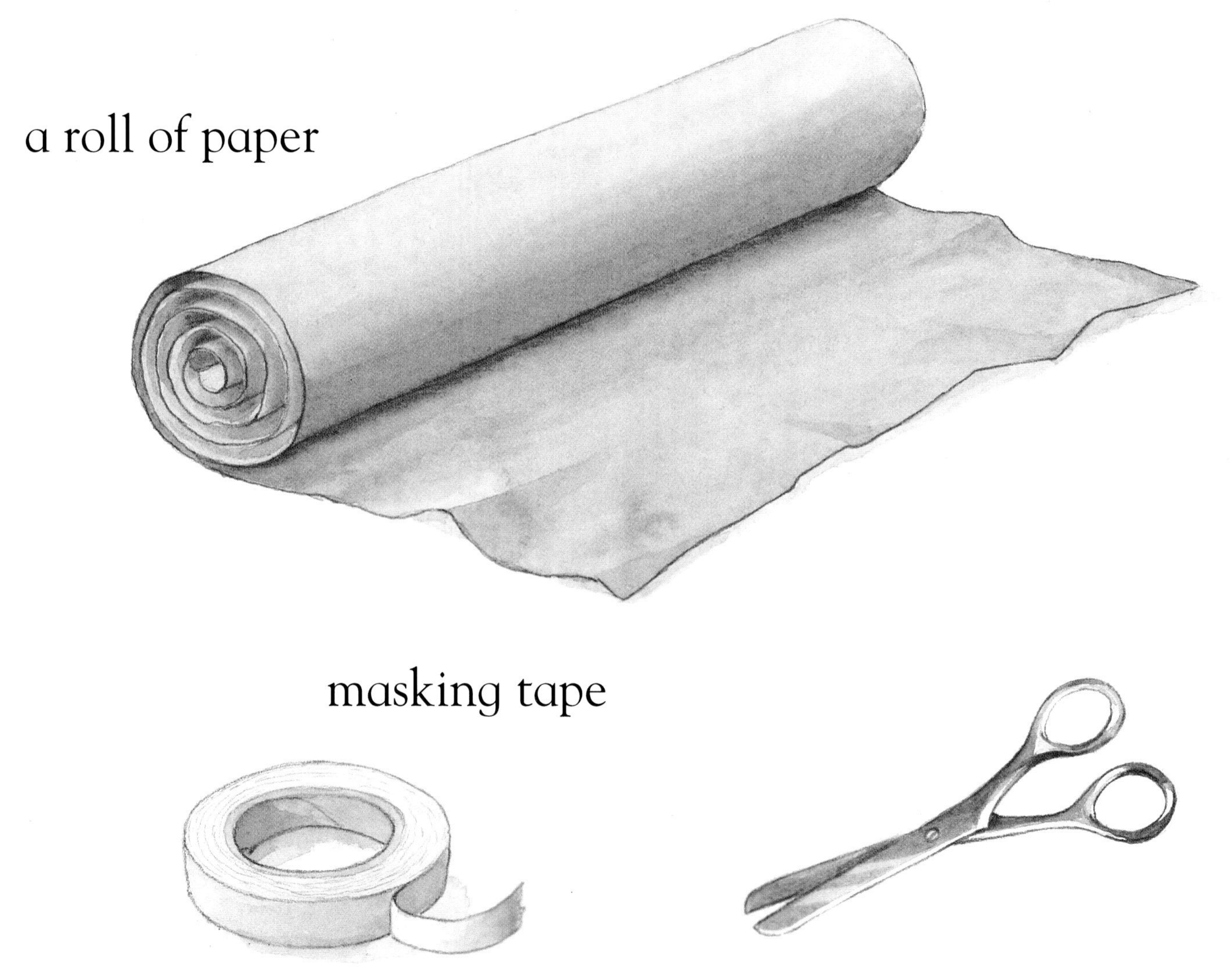

masking tape

and a pair of scissors.

Before they get started, Harvey has to cover the floor and the bench with paper. Otherwise they'll be covered with paint. But where has the tape gone?

Here it is! Silly Chip.

Harvey and Chip need aprons, too.
Painting is messy!

First they have to paint the cupboard with primer. Harvey looks in his big box of painting materials and finds

some primer

two paintbrushes

and a few sticks.

The primer stops the wood from showing through the paint. The sticks support the wood so Harvey and Chip can paint every bit of it.

When the primer is dry, Harvey takes out

white paint

and blue paint.

Chip paints the inside of the
cupboard with the white paint.
Harvey paints the outside with the blue paint.

Then Harvey takes out

yellow paint

and red paint.

Chip paints one door bright yellow. Harvey paints the other door bright red.

Next, they have to paint the top and bottom of the cupboard. Harvey takes out

a tin of black paint

and pours some into a jar for Chip.

Chip paints the top, and Harvey paints the bottom. It's hard to paint neatly, but Harvey has a steady hand. Little Chip has to use two hands to hold the brush!

They've used blue paint, white paint, yellow paint, red paint and black paint. That's all the paint Harvey has. But they still haven't done the shelves!
Chip wants to paint them green – but they don't have any green paint.
Harvey has an idea…

Harvey can mix the yellow paint with the blue paint
to make green paint! He takes

the yellow paint and the blue paint

and mixes them in a pot.

That's amazing! Harvey has made green paint by mixing the yellow and blue paint together.

Now Chip can paint the shelves green after all!

At last, the whole cupboard is painted. But so is Chip! It looks like the paintbrushes aren't the only things that need to be cleaned!

Make sure Chip is squeaky clean, Harvey!

It’s late – time for Chip to go home.
He’ll be back tomorrow.
In the meantime, Harvey still has work to do.

Later that night, when the paint is dry, Harvey puts the shelves in and screws the doors back on. What a long and busy day it has been!

The next morning, Chip doesn't come back.
Harvey waits all morning, but there's no sign of him.
Where can he be?

Here he is! Hurrah!

But he's covered in paint! What has he been doing?

He's made a present for Harvey!
It's a beautiful box. Chip has painted it blue,
yellow and his favourite colour, green.

Harvey is delighted. He can keep his brushes in it. And that gives him an idea. Now he knows what to put in his cupboard!

Fantastic! The paint-pots fit perfectly in the cupboard, and so do the brushes. It looks so neat and tidy. And after all that hard work, it's time for pink lemonade and buns!

Painting
Stuff

Harvey's Painting Tips

Paint
Harvey and Chip use water-soluble paint. It dries quickly, and it washes off with water, so it's easy to clean paintbrushes and to clean the painter!

In case of splashes

Harvey uses special paper from a hardware store, but you can use newspaper or plastic. The important thing is to avoid getting paint on everything!

Painting straight lines
If you have to paint in straight lines, use masking tape. For instance, if you want to paint something red and blue, follow the steps below.

Paint Carefully

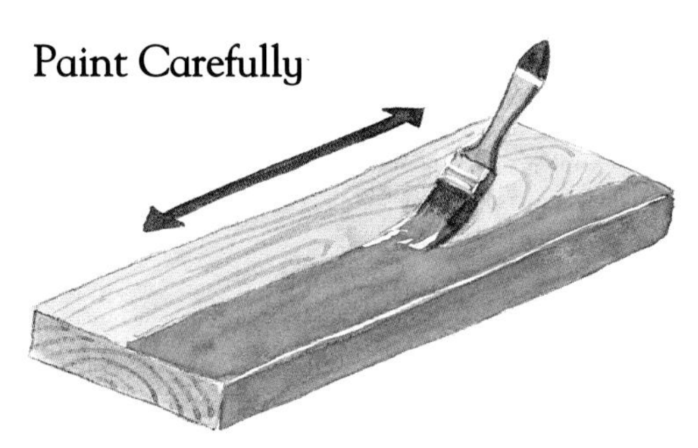

The bristles leave marks in the paint. If you are painting wood, try to follow the grain of the wood. Take it slowly!
If you have to apply more than one coat of paint, let it dry properly first. Otherwise it will go patchy and be very ugly.

Wash the Brushes!
Harvey and Chip washed the brushes carefully every time they changed to a different colour, as well as when they had finished painting. The next time they paint anything, the brushes will already be clean!

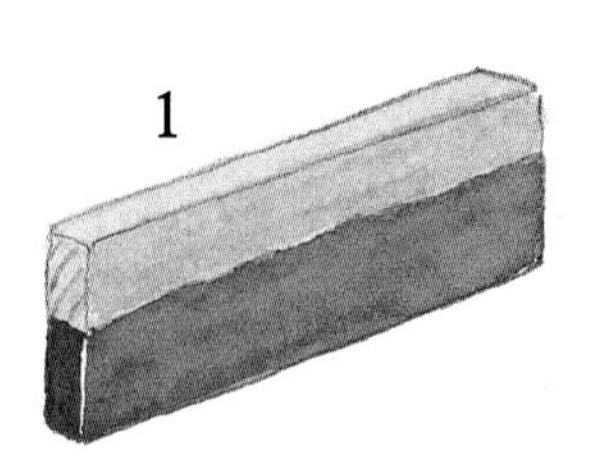

Paint the blue side first. Don't worry about getting blue paint on the other side.

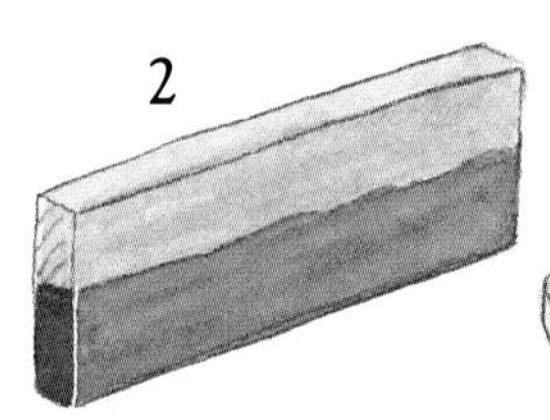

Let it dry properly!

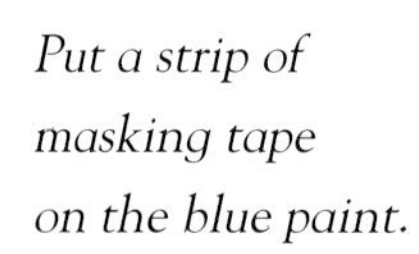

3

Put a strip of masking tape on the blue paint.

4

Paint the other side red. Go right up to the edge of the masking tape, so there isn't a gap. You can paint over the masking tape.

5

Peel off the masking tape carefully. Don't wait for the paint to dry!

Harvey's Colour Chart

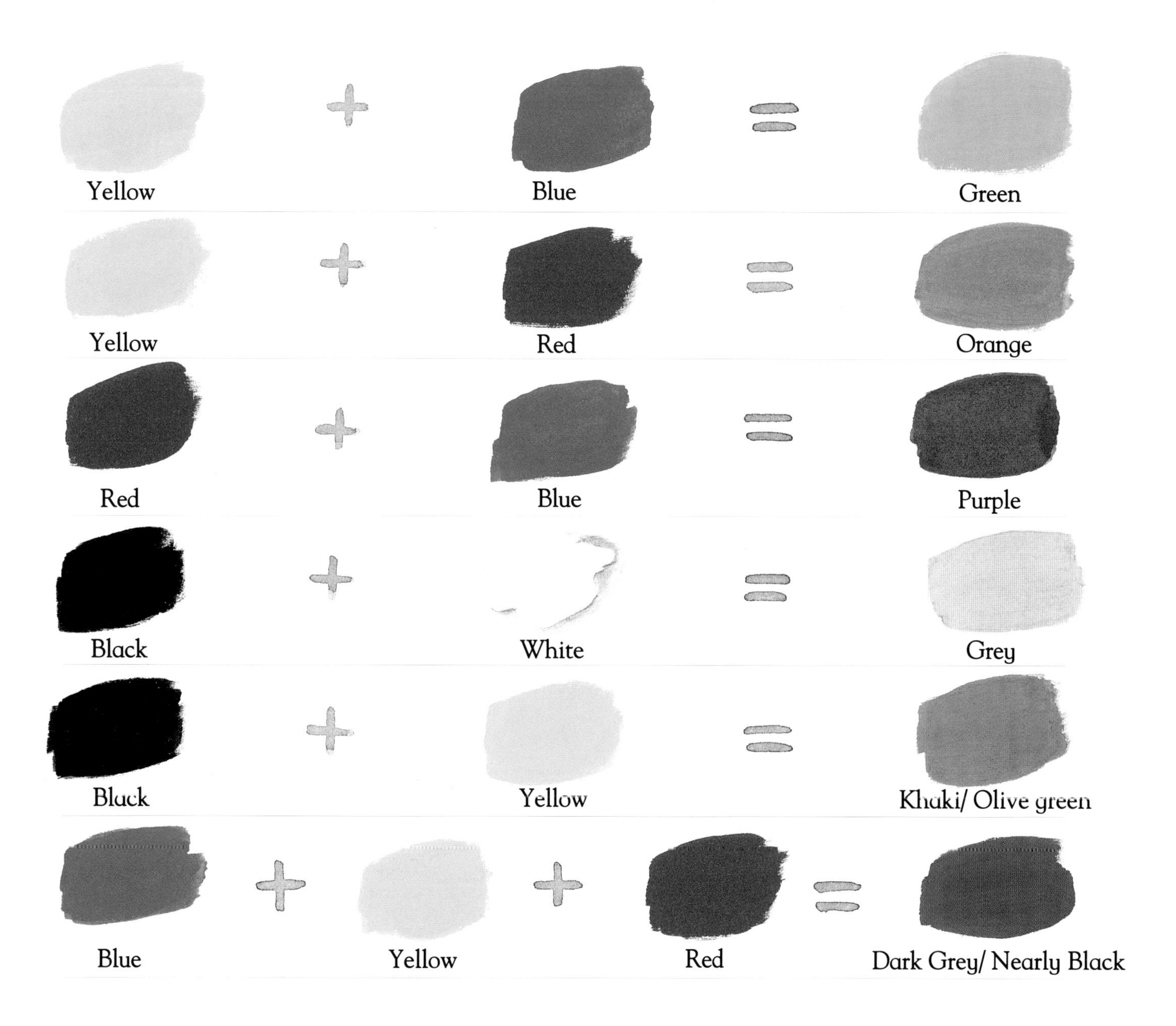

Why don't you try mixing different colours together? You can make even more colours by using more or less of one colour than the other – try it out and see what happens!

The End